For Marissa, Eva and Jonathan, with love.
M.B

For my mum and dad.
N.M

SNIP SNAP!
by Mara Bergman and Nick Maland
British Library Cataloguing in Publication Data
A catalogue record of this book is available from the British Library.

ISBN 0 340 88215 8 (HB)

Text copyright © Mara Bergman 2005
Illustrations copyright © Nick Maland 2005

First edition published 2005
10 9 8 7 6 5 4 3 2 1

Published by Hodder Children's Books
a division of Hodder Headline Limited
338 Euston Road London NW1 3BH

Printed in China

The illustrations in this book were made with watercolour on photocopied drawings.

Snip Snap!

Written by Mara Bergman * Illustrated by Nick Maland

Hodder
Children's
Books

A division of Hodder Headline Limited

When the alligator
came *creeping*...
creeping...

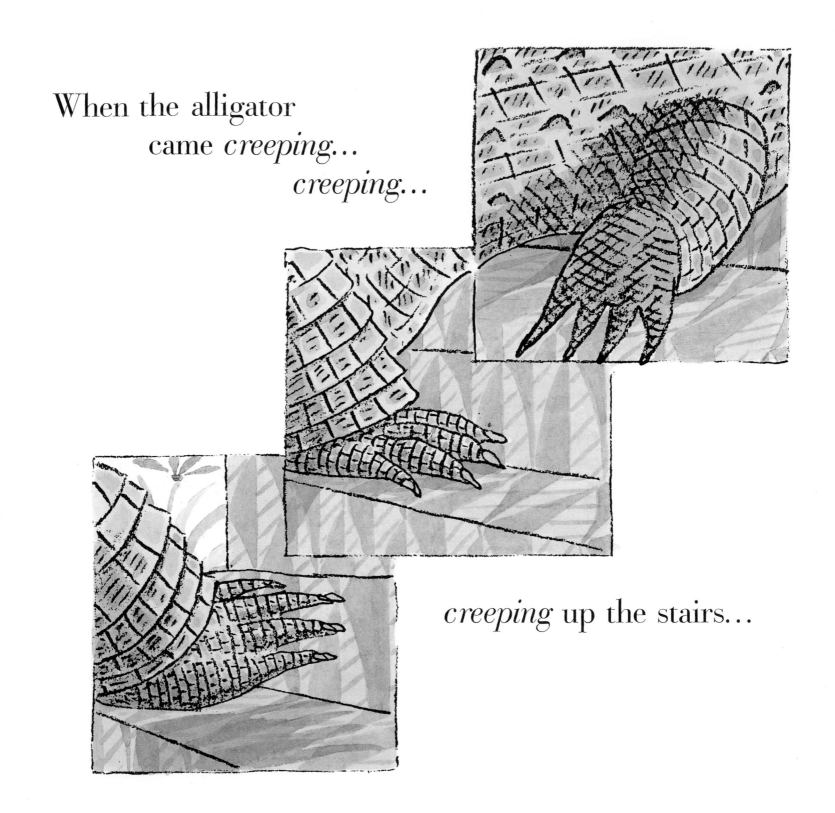

creeping up the stairs...

...were the children scared?

YOU BET THEY WERE!

Marissa tried to close the door.
Eva tried and tried some more.
And Jonathan didn't try at all,
he just cried and cried and cried...

...then he hid.

The alligator's mouth was wide.
Its teeth were long.
Its jaws were strong.
The children watched as it began
to bite the edges of the door.

SNIP SNAP
SNIP SNAP
snip snap snip
snap snip!

Were the children scared?

YOU BET
THEY WERE!

The alligator *slithered...*
slithered...
slithered
down the hall –

and slipped into the sitting room.

It *swishhhhhhed* and *swooooooshed* its tremendous tail, which was shiny and spiked and full of scales.

Were the children scared?

YOU BET THEY WERE!

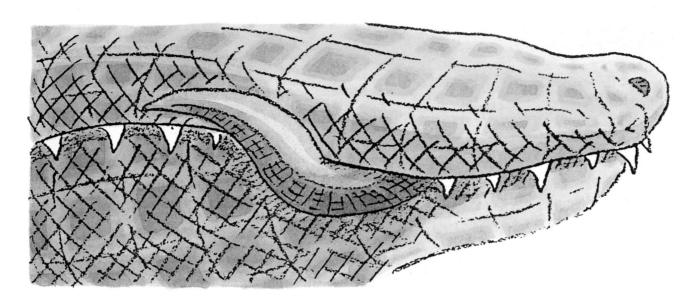

The alligator's tongue was flicking.

The alligator's feet were kicking.

Then the alligator's mouth
opened up v-e-r-y wide
creak…creak…creak…

as if to invite the children inside.

Were the children scared?

YOU BET
THEY WERE!

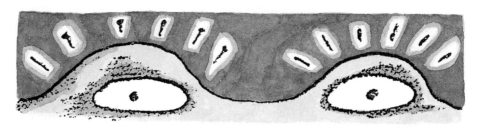

The alligator's eyes were flashing.

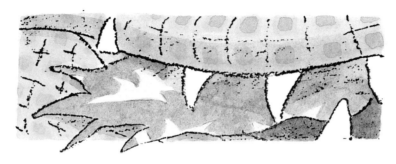

The alligator's teeth were gnashing
as tables and chairs and piano went crashing.

And after the sofa and curtains were ripped
the alligator licked its lips.

Were the children scared?

YOU BET THEY WERE!

And then what did the alligator do?
Did it say to the children,
'I'm going to eat you?'

Well, not exactly, but…

it came closer…

and closer…

and closer until…

The children decided they'd had enough
of all this scary alligator stuff.
They plucked up their courage
and gave a great shout:

'ALLIG

YOU

GET C

ATOR,

JT!'

And was the alligator scared?

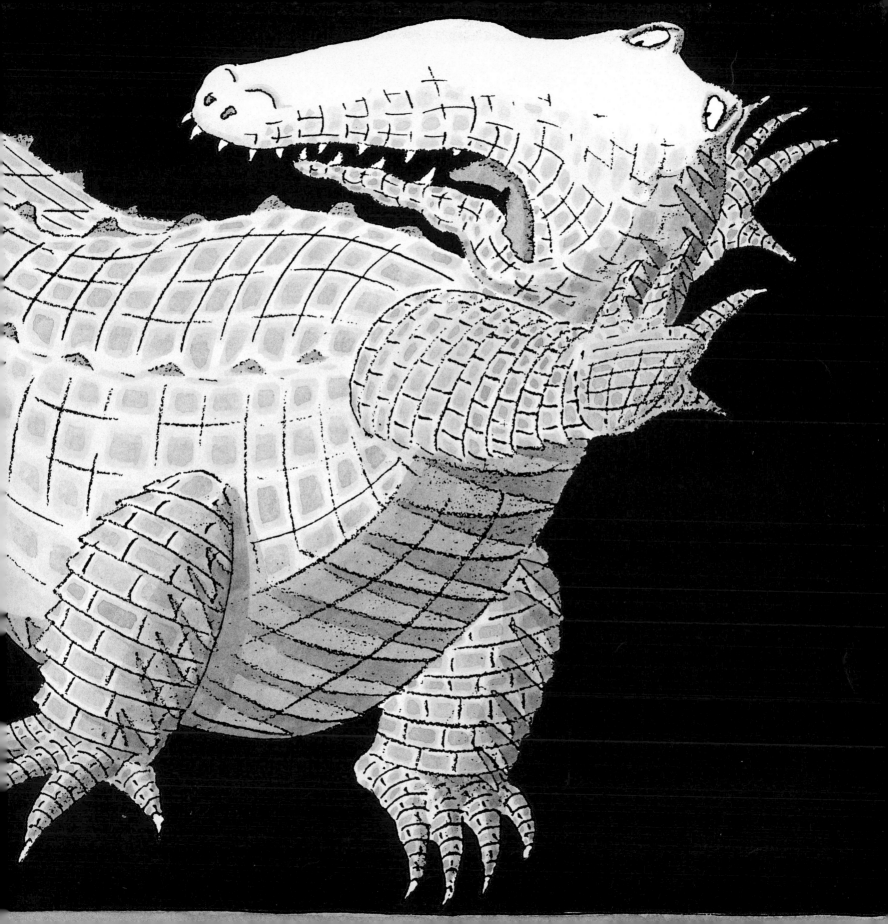

Thump bump

bump

thump!

...all the way home!